D0681233

All Paws Lead Home

Chloe's Quest

By Susan Levinsohn

Cover illustration by Jane Tasciotti

Chloe photo by Tye Studios

A portion of the proceeds from this book will go to

Sheltie Rescue

Dedication

To my special Shelties Skylar and Chloe, who taught me patience, devotion and especially what it is to love and be loved unconditionally.

"He is your friend, your partner, your defender, your dog.

You are his life, his love, his leader. He will be yours, faithful and true, to the last beat of his heart.

You owe it to him to be worthy of such devotion"

-Author Unknown

INTRODUCTION

"Mom, Dad……wake up! Please, wake up. I can't find Skylar. You know we always jump on the bed together to wake you up in the morning. I'm really worried mom".

And so began my journey after the loss of my brother and best friend, Skylar.

You could say I'm a very lucky girl. I have loving parents who spoil me, a nice house to live in with lots of toys and pillows and a wonderful yard where I play. I even see horses ride by from time to time up on the ridge behind our house.

It took a while for me to learn to enjoy these things alone because I really missed my brother, Skylar. I don't know where he went, and though mom always gave me lots of love and attention, I could tell she was really sad sometimes. She must have missed Skylar too.

By the way, my name is Chloe and I'm a dog.

1

There is a lot to tell you about Ginger, my new sister. I used to be the one to get all the attention and even when we went on walks through the neighborhood, people would stop to pet me and tell me how beautiful I was. But then it changed and, Ginger started to get most of the attention. You see, Ginger is...........special.

I guess it would help if I started at the beginning.

I remember being surrounded by lots of dogs and other puppies and it was really hot because we were all kept in a large pen together outside. It wasn't a great place to be, especially when you live in Florida in the summer. I was smaller than all the other dogs, even the ones that were my age, and I was always getting picked on and pounced on and even got bitten sometimes with the needle sharp teeth of the other puppies. I didn't like it much, always looking for a quiet corner to be by myself.

There's not a lot I remember about the place I came from but I do recall the time someone picked me up and carried me away from all the other puppies. I'm not really sure where we went or what happened, but when I woke up, I was back in the hot pen with all the other dogs and boy, was my throat hurting. It hurt a lot.

As I began looking for a quiet spot one day to get out of the heat as much as possible, I remember being picked up once again, put in a large truck, inside a crate and then driving for a pretty long time even though I can't tell you for exactly how long. I tried to sleep because, even though there were other dogs with me, most of them older, I was enjoying being in a cooler place and having my own space.

It appears that I came from a place where they kept breeding lots of dogs, keeping only the ones for show; kind of like a beauty contest. They wanted the best and prettiest ones and all I know is that they didn't want me. I was smaller than the others, as I mentioned, but worse than that, I had a crooked jaw that gave me kind of a lopsided grin with one tooth sticking straight out on one side of my mouth and two teeth that crossed over each other on the other side. No beauty contest could be won looking like that!

So, as I later learned, that was why I was being taken on the long drive, in the crate, in the truck. I was travelling to my new home.

We finally arrived at our destination, after what seemed like hours of driving. It was a large fairground in a place called Davie, Florida and I was so happy to get out of my crate, out of the truck and I really needed to go potty. But when I got out, I was completely overwhelmed. There were people and dogs everywhere, with a lot of talking, laughing out loud, music playing and lots of barking. It took every ounce of control to keep from trying to jump right back into that truck and into my crate. Of course, I was way too small to even get close to reaching the first step into the truck but I was willing to give it a try because all I could think was, please, please don't let this be my new home.

Everything happened pretty fast then; I was very confused and, I admit, frightened. People were all around us and strange dogs kept coming over to sniff me. Then a lady walked towards us, came right up to me, bending down real low and started speaking very softly to me, almost in baby talk. She then put something around my neck and began to tug lightly. I fought back for a bit but when I saw she was trying to lead me away from all the craziness and confusion, I decided to follow. We walked through all the crowds and then she picked me up and put me in a car.

I wasn't looking forward to another long ride and I was so scared and in all the confusion I forgot to go so, I had no choice but to do it right there. Right there in the lady's car.

I was ashamed that I couldn't control myself but before I knew it, we were getting out of the car in front of a nice house. The lady didn't even seem to mind that I urinated all over her back seat and just picked me up and set me down on the ground where I then noticed a tall man with a dog next to him. The man had a big smile on his face and the dog looked kind of like me but was a little bigger and had different colors to his fluffy coat.

Skylar and I met for the first time.

After greeting each other in the front yard, we took a short walk and then we all went into, what was to be, my new home. Of course, I had to check everything out and my new mom and dad just stood back and let me wander from room to room while Skylar followed me, though I'm not sure why. Was he curious about me or worried about me being in his house?

2

As time went on, one thing was for certain. Life was grand. It is every dog's dream to grow up in such a loving and caring home and with a brother, and best friend, like Skylar. Right from the start, I became the special one, though I don't mean "special" in the same way that we referred to Ginger later on.

My new mom and dad loved everything about me including my crooked smile with the crazy tooth sticking straight out. And they didn't even mind that I couldn't bark out loud like Skylar and other dogs. You see, I had actually had my vocal chords cut so I wouldn't make a lot of noise. I guess that explains the sore throat I had. I don't really understand it, but there was nothing wrong with me and the only reason this was done, was to keep me quiet. For heaven's sake, if you don't want a dog to bark, don't get a dog! It is our way to communicate, so now what do I do? And later in life I started to have trouble breathing a little and I was always choking like something was stuck in my throat.

A few days after I had arrived, my new mom found out about my inability to bark like other dogs. You see, I was very quiet for the first few days, being kind of nervous in a new home and all, but when she accidentally stepped on my paw and she heard me bark, out came this raspy, hoarse sound. I guess she thought I was sick or something because she immediately called someone on the phone and I heard her yell really loud and she said she would never give me back!

On that day, at that moment, I realized I loved my new mom.

I quickly figured out that if I simply smiled my crooked smile, and looked up at mom and dad with my big brown, button eyes, that I could, and would, get just about anything. They had a sectional sofa where I would lie up on the back cushions and look out of both windows into the yard and out onto the ridge. And my pillow! Oh, how I loved my pillow. Actually, I love all pillows…….to jump up on the sofa and then push and move them so they are just right, and then lay my head on them. But my favorite, the one bought just for me, has different doggie pictures on it (I think one sort of looks like me) and it says W O O F. Did I mention that I love my pillow?

And Skylar. Skylar became my best friend and did everything for me, too. He showed me around my new house and taught me where the coolest spots were to take our naps, which came in handy in the South Florida heat. He would stand at the back door and bark to me, telling me to follow him outside where we would run and play in the yard and watch people walk by and sometimes the horses gallop by up on the ridge. We would pretend to chase them. He helped me meet all the nice dogs, children and people in the neighborhood. While Skylar was very friendly, always happy to see them all, I was a bit shyer and would say hello but that was about it. I learned to follow Skylar everywhere and do whatever he did, not having to think about anything. With everyone taking such good care of me, I simply soaked up all the love and attention. This was the life. It was all about me. What was also pretty great was that Skylar even let me take his bone right out of his mouth if I wanted it. I was the princess.

We would get together when mom and dad were at work and, while we mostly napped or sat on the sofa looking out at the ridge, we sometimes would get ourselves into trouble. Either it was paper and stuff from the bathroom garbage cans, or we would find clothes in the laundry basket (if the door was left open) and pull them out to lay on, and a couple of times we even chewed the corner of mom's favorite chair. We never admitted which one of us did it. It was our secret. And we always did it before, or after, Aunt Toni came by or mom and dad got home.

See mom didn't like to leave us alone all day while she was at work, so Aunt Toni came to take care of us. We loved Aunt Toni. We would all go for long walks together or just sit in the front yard and get brushed and always got lots of love. It was our special time.

Life was grand!

3

Seven years past, and it was early October with the cooling down of the temperatures which was welcome after the scorching heat of the summer. With all our furry, thick coats, we tried not to go outside in that heat for too long. Thank goodness my dad liked to keep the house cold and that Skylar had taught me all the best and coolest places to nap.

I remember that particular October because that is when Skylar got sick. Mom, who used to be at work all day, was suddenly home a lot more, which I loved, because if I wasn't following Skylar around, I was following mom. But we weren't having fun together like we always did. Instead we started going to the vet's office a lot more and not always the same one. I was getting bored on these trips, just wanting to be home so we could play and run in the yard, chasing the horses and people up on the ridge. And why was he sick anyway? None of them could tell mom what was wrong with Skylar.

On one of our trips, we walked into this really cool house where there were people and dogs and even some cats and a baby opossum. It looked like a really fun place and everyone was just sitting around together on comfy sofas. There were pillows! I later learned that this was yet another new vet but this ended up being different from the others because it was when we met Doc Joyce. Mom really liked her and I liked getting to say hello to all the people there because they would pet me and tell me how beautiful I was. I was never that interested in other dogs, except Skylar, though I might say hi to a few of them just out of curiosity, but I certainly didn't want to play with them. We ended up making quite a few trips to see Doc Joyce and they were doing lots of tests on poor Skylar; I could tell he really didn't like it but on one of our visits, Doc sat down with mom, while I was curled up on the sofa with 3 pillows.

I could tell mom didn't like hearing what Doc had to say, and she cried and then Doc Joyce gave her a hug.

My world really turned upside down because Skylar wasn't looking out for me anymore, or calling me to run outside and play and watch the people and horses. Mom wasn't paying too much attention to me either except to take me on my walks or feed me. Oh sure, she still scratched behind my ears, my favorite spot or sat with me in the yard, but I knew.........I could sense she was worrying about Skylar.

So, for the next few months, we were either taking Skylar to see Doc Joyce or Aunt Toni was coming to the house but not to take us for walks or brush our hair. She came almost every day to give Skylar special medicine while mom would be mashing up this strange food, trying to make Skylar eat.

I could tell he wasn't hungry and just wanted to go lay outside on the patio next to the pool. He would lay in the same place, though once in a while he would walk over to the fence and look out over the ridge. I would watch him just stand there and stare, almost as if he wanted to run back and forth with me chasing the horses, but all he could do was look out and remember how fun it was.

What was happening? Skylar was sick and no one was worrying about me. No one was playing with me or looking out for me. Did you all forget that I am the special one?

Mom called to me and put on my leash and said she and I were going for a walk together. Just the two of us. Oh how excited I was to have some special time together, but while we did take a short walk, mom brought me over to her friend's house. I liked it there because her daughter, Annabel, loved to brush my hair and give me hugs and was always so happy to see me. I ran right over to her and didn't even notice when mom left. I just spent special time with Annabel enjoying all the attention, hearing how pretty and soft I was. She really liked my paws too because she thought they looked like mittens.

After some time, I got tired and went off to sleep in a corner of the sofa on a nice pillow, though it wasn't my pillow. The next thing I knew, mom was back and we walked home together. She put me in my bed, right next to hers, gave me my special treat, and we went to sleep.

When I woke up the next morning, I immediately went to wake up Skylar because I was always the first one up, but I couldn't find him anywhere. I didn't know where he was.

4

It was really hard with him being gone and I just didn't understand why he went away. I barked a lot, in my raspy whisper-like way, because I just didn't know what to do. He always showed me where to go and when to play. I was feeling so lost and alone.

Mom tried to get me to follow her outside in the yard to run and play when she got back from work, but it just wasn't the same. We went for walks, visited with all the other dogs in the neighborhood, but they didn't interest me that much, other than to say a quick hello. So, I started to spend a lot of time alone in the yard.

As I was dozing under the shade of the lugustrum tree one afternoon, I noticed something flying high above, over the ridge, swooping down low to the ground and then soaring up high again into the sky. I watched it for a long time only to realize it was a hawk. He was very beautiful and graceful and I noticed that he had very good eyesight. He could see the smallest things on the ground from so high up in the sky and then would swoop down faster than anything I had ever seen, picking up whatever he found in the tall grass and fly away. I watched him for days and even tried to run and jump and fly off to join him because it looked like such fun, but I barely got all four paws off the ground at the same time. I guess flying was out of the question for me so, I would just have to watch him, and run and jump and dream.

How come I never noticed this hawk before? So my new routine was to go outside into the yard whenever I could. I would run to sit under the shade of the tree and watch for the beautiful hawk soaring through the sky on his hunt.

While waiting for my new feathered friend one afternoon, I decided to sniff around the bushes and flowerbeds, when I came face to face with the oddest fellow. It was an iguana and while strange, he was also very beautiful in his bright green skin. I stopped and quietly watched him for a while as he was sunning himself next to the pool, then decided to go investigate but as soon as I moved in closer to introduce myself, he dove straight into the water. I stepped back, losing my balance a bit, as he startled me, moving so quickly. Watching him I was amazed at what a good swimmer he was. He dove straight to the bottom and swam effortlessly across the entire length of the pool and I couldn't believe how long he could hold his breath under water. When he reached the far side, he crawled right out of the pool and up onto a big rock that was there.

Watching this odd, yet beautiful, iguana, I wished I could jump right in that pool with him and swim away.

And so days turned into weeks and as often as I could, I would go out into the yard and wait for my new friends to run and jump and chase after the hawk flying high over the ridge, dreaming of joining him. Or sit under the shade of the tree waiting for the iguana to appear and show off his water skills.

I was still feeling lonely and neglected so I decided to run away. I followed dad around when he was home and always knew when he was getting ready to leave for work so as he opened the door to the garage, I quietly followed him out, without him seeing me. He ran back in for a minute, I think he forgot something, I noticed the door was opened and it looked so nice outside and since no one really noticed me that much anymore, I decided it was a good time to just leave. I walked right out that garage door and headed down the street. I was looking to see if anyone was out to try and get some attention but the street was quiet so I kept on walking. Before I knew it, I was at Annabel's house. I walked up to the front door and barked to let her know I was there, but I don't think she was able to hear me with my raspy voice, so I decided to lie down and wait because she had to come out at some point. As I was dozing off, I heard someone calling my name, over and over so I picked up my head, and then tried to hide really fast. It was my dad and I didn't want him to see me. When he finally did, he came over to where I was hiding, picked me up and carried me home. I got lots of kisses and hugs and he didn't even seem too mad, which was good, but I really didn't want to go back home and be all alone. I was missing Skylar so much.

5

Resting my head on several pillows, I heard mom calling me, asking if I wanted to go for a ride in the car. It wasn't my favorite thing to do, but as long as I was with them, it was okay. We drove for a while and ended up at a building where I could see lots of people and dogs, and there was a large play area outside too, where dogs were running around playing together. So we all walked in together and........Wow. There were dogs everywhere, in all shapes, sizes, colors, and I really liked seeing them. I pressed my nose up to the glass and some of the dogs even tried to lick it.....right through the glass.

After walking around for a while, we went into this small room. The door opened and in walked a lady carrying a dog, and she was pretty cute, even with her funny looking hair all chopped up. I went over to say hello because she was just standing there looking pretty scared, but just as I approached her, she looked me right in the eye and started to jump in the air and spin in circles and run around the room. The nice lady tried really hard to catch her to calm her down, but it wasn't working very well and she kept laughing. When she finally got hold of the dog, I had to chuckle to myself because all you saw was the dogs rear end sticking straight up in the ladies arms with its back legs going a mile a minute in the air like she was still running somewhere, and you couldn't see her head.

Dad was sitting really quiet in a chair so I decided to go and hide behind him because I was a little afraid that she would get away from the lady again and I didn't want to be knocked over with her running around so out of control. I wasn't sure what made her start running in the first place, but I didn't really like it and anyway, I thought we were there too long and I wanted to go home.

Everyone got up, the lady took the dog away and we all got to leave that small room. I think mom and dad felt bad for me because we walked over to this neat area where they picked out some special treats and a new leash……all I could think of was how pretty I was going to look wearing that!

I was even happier when we finally got in the car so we could get out of that place and go home. But I'm not alone. What was SHE doing there? I immediately went and curled up way in the back of dad's SUV while mom was saying how the dog must be overly excited after being so cooped up, whatever that meant. As we pulled out of the parking lot, mom came into the back with us, took hold of the dogs face and said, "I think I'll call you Ginger." Then she kissed her on the nose. Hey, what about me?

We drove home.

6

Right from the start, I knew I was in trouble. While at first I was willing to give Ginger a chance at being a part of my world, I soon realized that this wasn't going to happen. She was not, at all, like other dogs I had known and certainly not even close to being like Skylar.

That first night with her seemed like it would never end. At first I thought everything would be okay because mom put Ginger in a crate with a bed, a toy and gave her a treat as I got to go where I always went; in my bed right next to mom. But none of us got much sleep that night because she wouldn't stop barking or crying. The later it got, the more upset I got as did mom. At one point I saw that mom actually fell asleep sitting on the floor next to Ginger's crate. I had to nap pretty much the whole next day!

When I first came to live here, I recall how shy and quiet I was for the first few days, trying to get used to all the new surroundings and new smells, but not Ginger. She was just the opposite. It was like someone wound her up, sort of like a wind- up toy, let her go and she just kept spinning. From morning to night she ran around the house barking and crying or ran in circles around the dining table or kitchen island, and when she started to get tired, she slowed down from a run to a walk and then would rev right back up again.

No matter what mom did, Ginger would have no part of it, didn't listen to her or pay attention to anything. When she wasn't running in circles or barking, she would just all of a sudden stop. She just stopped and stood perfectly still, looking into space with this terrified look on her face with ears back and tail between her legs. This went on for days and I realized that I wanted no part of her or this crazy behavior so would bark at mom, in my whisper voice, to go outside in the yard just wanting to be alone because Ginger was exhausting and she wasn't very nice to me either. Maybe my friends would be there to cheer me up.

On a few occasions mom let us both out in the yard together but all Ginger did was run around in her crazy way and if I got even a little close to her, she would bite my head and ears when all I wanted to do was watch the people and horses go by. But Ginger just barked and ran around in circles so much that there wasn't any grass left, just dirt.

Mom always came to help me and brought us both inside where I would jump right up on the sofa and lay down in the corner. This became my safe place. I decided to stay away from Ginger and pretend she wasn't even there, as much as I could anyway, though I did peek at her every now and then. My favorite part of the day became bed time when she was in her crate and I got to be with mom and dad alone. They would bring me up on their bed and cuddle with me telling me what a good girl I was, before I went to sleep.

There was nothing Ginger would learn no matter how hard mom tried to teach her. It was easy for me when I was that young and because there was always a treat involved. I did whatever I was asked to do and had a hard time understanding why she didn't want to learn.

Over the next few weeks, a lady showed up at the house at different times and seemed to be there to help teach Ginger things but, of course, she wanted no part of it. She would just stand there with her head down, ears back and tail between her legs. After a while the lady didn't come to the house anymore.

Getting into the car one afternoon, I got excited because I was really hoping we were taking Ginger back to where she came from. Maybe we could pick out a nicer and calmer dog. But that wasn't the case. We went to see Doc Joyce and when we walked in, everyone there was excited to see mom and the "new dog", and of course, I was completely overlooked. So while Doc was checking out Ginger and talking to mom, I jumped up on the sofa and curled up in the corner on a pillow. It annoyed me that someone left their purse right where I wanted to lay but, because I really am a sweet girl and courteous, I decided not to knock it off and just used part of it as a pillow.

I heard mom explaining to Doc that Ginger had been found running around the streets of Miami all by herself and then brought to the Shelter by someone, which is where we found her. I can only imagine how scary that must have been for her with all the noise, people and cars with no bed to sleep in and probably not much food either because she was really skinny underneath that chopped up haircut. She also told her that Ginger was afraid of everything; people, noises, the yard man……everything. Mom couldn't use a hairdryer, the washing machine or anything that made noise or it would send Ginger into a tailspin. She would even go nuts when mom tried to open a can and it wasn't even the kind of opener you have to plug in. Oh, and the rain! It didn't matter if it was 2 drops or a whole lot; and forget about thunder. I would be happy just to go take a nap but not Ginger. She would start to run even faster, bark even louder, cry and run to the doors and scratch at them. I stayed far away from her in my spot on the sofa.

Mom explained all this to Doc so she gave her some medicine for Ginger and said it would calm her down. It didn't. And I pretty much knew by now, that Ginger was staying with us because she got lots of toys and of course I didn't like any of them. She even got her own bed. And yes, the new leash was for her, not me.

Ginger started getting her new medicine every day and mom tried to teach her things but it didn't work. She continued to just run around in circles; I now called it the Circle Dance.

And so went our days and weeks and months. So much time was being spent on the new dog and I wasn't getting any attention. Even when I would go out into the backyard, I couldn't find my friends. They were gone and I think Ginger chased them away. I wished Ginger would go away.

Our morning walks were one thing I looked forward to, because I got to be with mom, and Ginger seemed to like it. We would start walking through the neighborhood first, then turn into the park where there were always great things to smell and see. Next, we would head up onto the ridge where we could see our house when we reached the top of the hill. We came face to face with some horses on one of our walks; I bet they were the ones I watched so often from my yard, but I'm not really sure. And we sometimes met nice people too, and I would always say hello to them but Ginger didn't because she was too afraid and would hide behind mom.

What I found interesting, was that Ginger seemed to like other dogs. It was sure obvious that she liked them more than she liked me. She would walk right up to them and say hello though she wouldn't play with them, even if they wanted to. But she wasn't afraid. Then, on one of our walks through the neighborhood, we got to meet a new dog whose name was Milo. He seemed nice, though a lot bigger than we were and his hair just about covered his eyes. Mom was about to let us go and say hello when the people told her that Milo didn't like other dogs too much so just as she started pulling us away from him, out of nowhere, he and Ginger started to play together. They were running and rolling around in the grass and it was the first time I ever saw Ginger having fun. Everyone seemed surprised by this so they let them both keep on playing together because they were having such a good time and seemed to really like each other. From that day on, when mom took us for our morning walk, Ginger would always stop right in front of Milo's house and try to walk up to the front door like she thought she could ring the bell and ask him to come out and play. How did she remember where he lived?

We started to see Milo almost every day and he and Ginger would have the best time playing together and I could see that she was a tough little dog because Milo would sometimes knock her down but she would get right back up and then pounce on his back and bite his ears and his neck, but she wasn't being mean like she was with me. I would just lie in the grass.

There was something special between Ginger and Milo that I didn't understand. Not only did she know where Milo lived but he would often be sitting right outside our fence in the back yard waiting for her. At first I had no idea how he got there but then his owners told mom that he kept digging a hole under their fence and running away but they always knew where to find him. Milo and Ginger knew how to find each other.

A week or so later, on one of our morning walks, we got to meet yet another new dog to the neighborhood. It seemed Annabel's mom decided to rescue a dog for their family and her name was Daisy.

Daisy came to stay with us once when her mom had to go away, and she found a spot next to the sofa on the floor. She didn't move from there the whole time except to go for a walk. She seemed afraid not even wanting to get up and eat until we all went to bed at night and she was sure no one was watching. I left her alone and almost forgot she was even there but not Ginger. She kept trying to go over to Daisy and would stand there and just stare at her or lay down next to her almost as if she knew Daisy was afraid and needed company.

Ginger seemed very upset the day Daisy went home. She kept going to the place next to the sofa where Daisy had been and would make these strange little crying noises. By then, I was used to hearing her cry so didn't pay much attention. Mom knew she was upset so the next day, we all went over to Daisy's house. Once inside, I could see Daisy in the back room, just lying there in a bed. I immediately looked for Annabel, but I think she was at school. Ginger was trying to pull on her leash and get out the door but then she noticed Daisy in her bed. When she did, she pulled on the leash so hard that it slipped right out of mom's hand and off she ran right to where Daisy was, jumped right in bed with her and the two of them started to roll around and play. Mom and her friend were laughing and seemed so happy that they were having fun. I went to lie in the kitchen by myself.

What was it about Milo and now Daisy that Ginger liked so much? There were other friendly dogs we knew, ones I liked much better, but not Ginger. These three were all different.

From always being the center of attention, I was now reduced to an after-thought most of the time so I had to create my moments. One of my favorite ones became getting up early with dad every morning, while mom and Ginger slept in. We would take a walk together first and then I would get to share some strawberries with him while he ate his breakfast. It was a very special time for me but it didn't last long because once mom woke up, Ginger got up too and then it all would start again; the barking, the running, the crying..........and mom giving all the attention to her..........okay, time to jump up on the sofa.

7

Months passed, and things didn't settle down. Lost in my own little world most of the time, I greedily accepted any ounce of attention and dreamed of the day life would become "normal" again.

Wait……was this the day? A special lady doctor came to the house one afternoon and at first I figured it was just another new person to try and help mom with Ginger. But this lady seemed a little different right from the start. She didn't try and teach Ginger things but only just sat there with mom and watched or followed her at a distance as Ginger did her thing around the house. She was there for a really long time……….watching……….and talking to mom and writing lots of notes. Then she gave some medicine to mom and told her that Ginger would have to take it every day and that she was convinced things would get better. I wanted to tell her to forget it. But mom thanked the doctor and the next morning, started giving Ginger her new medicine. It was okay with me because I always managed to get a little treat at the same time, once I gave mom "the look"........guilt is a wonderful thing sometimes.

Secretly, I was hoping for a miracle but I didn't notice any difference in Ginger..........at least not right away. Mom continued to try and work with her every day and the biggest challenge was to just get her to lay still on a mat while dropping treats for her. Nothing seemed easy for Ginger.

Gradually, she started to stay on her mat for longer periods of time. And a few times she actually came to mom for a treat when she heard "leave it", would now sit when told to, and wasn't running as much, and........she was getting a little fat. Too many treats, I guess, but mom kept at it with her. Showing me a trick one morning, I really didn't want to do it, but I knew that if I pretended to try and then give mom "the look", that I would get a treat anyway. But wait.......what's this? Ginger had been watching us and then did the trick. Mom asked her to do it again, and she did. Ginger started learning lots of new tricks and I realized that she was very smart and learned very fast. In my defense, even though I'm pretty smart, at my age I really only want to do what I want to do.

8

On a grey, rainy day, as I lay on the sofa on my pillow, taking my afternoon nap with mom next to me reading a book, out of nowhere Ginger came running over, jumped on the sofa right into mom's lap and just started giving her kisses, making these little noises I had never heard; almost like a baby. Mom put her arms around her and started to cry, though I have no idea why. Once I was satisfied that she was okay, I turned around to face the opposite direction, because Ginger was now in my space, and I didn't like it. Not one bit.

Other things started to change then too, like Ginger standing closer to people we saw on our walks, and even let the older lady down the street scratch her head. And while Milo and Daisy were still her special friends, Ginger started to play a little with other dogs as well, though she still didn't pay any attention to me. I did catch her sneaking up to me one day when I was taking a nap, trying to sniff at me but I pretended to be asleep.

And there were suddenly lots of new toys in the house. There were stuffed animals and creatures in every room because mom was teaching Ginger to grab hold of one of them whenever she got scared or nervous. There were even games with hidden food and, I tried once to get to the hidden treasure in one of the new games with no luck at all. But Ginger had them all figured out in no time, pushing this with her nose one way and pawing at that the other way and before you knew it, all the food was gone. She had to be smart AND get all the attention? And to make it worse, as we were settling into bed one night, I got into my bed like I always did waiting for my treat and here comes Ginger into the room with mom and crawls into a bed right next to mine. She sleeps there now.

I don't know how, but Ginger started to know when everything was supposed to happen. Like when it was time for a walk, or time to eat, or time to practice tricks, or go sit in the office with mom so she could do her work, and especially when it was time to go to bed. So, every day pretty much became like the day before and boy, did she get nervous if mom forgot!

The three of us took a ride in the car one afternoon to visit a friend of mom's and when we walked into the house it smelled really good. I think I smelled cookies baking. We all went to sit outside and I decided to run and join the children playing. As I started to follow them, expecting Ginger to barrel past me, I noticed she was walking over to a little boy who was sitting in a really funny looking chair with big wheels on it. I thought maybe she was going to get him to play also but instead, she just walked up to him, put her head right in his lap and stayed there. Even when his mom went to bring him a drink, Ginger didn't move. She just stayed there, with her head in his lap the whole time we visited and the little boy was smiling and scratching her head.

We would sometimes go back there and every time we did, I would play with the children in the yard or find a shady spot and take a nap, but Ginger would always stay right next to the little boy in the strange chair. I just couldn't figure out why she seemed to always make friends with dogs and now people that were different.

As time went on, I started getting lots more attention, mom seemed happier and Ginger was a little calmer. Oh, she still ran around the house and barked at everything but she seemed to not be as afraid. She followed mom into the laundry room and even let her use the hairdryer on her after a bath. And I began to soften a little towards her as well; we started to spend some time together and she actually wanted to play with me on a few occasions. Maybe she wasn't that bad after all.

9

Napping in the shade of the tree one afternoon, I heard our names being called to come inside so, I jumped right up and headed for the door. I was waiting for Ginger to come barreling past me but she never came, so I just went in. Mom kept calling her, then went out back only instead of bringing her in, I heard mom let out a scream. I went running to see what was happening only to find her running around calling Ginger's name. It appeared that the yard man must have left the back gate open and Ginger was gone.

Mom brought me inside then went out back again as I jumped up on the back cushion of the sofa so I could see what was going on. She ran out of the gate and onto the ridge, all the time calling for Ginger. She was gone for a long time and I was so happy when she finally came back but she didn't have Ginger with her.

She wrote a quick note and left it on the counter, gave me a treat, a hug and was out the door, locking it behind her. I heard the car start, then silence. I was alone.

Hours must have passed because it was getting dark and dad came home. I ran to greet him at the door as he started calling for Ginger, because we always raced to see who could get to dad first. I wanted to tell him that she was gone, but of course, I couldn't. He put his things down on the counter, saw the note mom left, and then grabbed the phone. When he hung up, he put on my leash and we walked all over the neighborhood, even going into people's back yards, which we never did. I was getting tired and my paws hurt.

When we got back to the house, mom was there. She gave me a hug and then she and dad took turns making phone calls telling everyone about Ginger missing and asking for their help. Mom and dad didn't sleep that night.

The next morning, before the sun was even up, mom left the house and drove away. Dad stayed with me and we did our normal routine of taking a walk, then sharing strawberries. It happened to be a really nice day, and there was a wonderful breeze blowing which always felt good, so I barked, as only I could, to go out in the yard. Dad opened the back door, and out I went.

I tried to do my part to help search for Ginger by going into all the bushes and flower beds, even though I knew mom wouldn't like it, but maybe Ginger was hiding somewhere. When I couldn't find her, I walked over to the fence and just started to bark. I barked for a pretty long time; maybe she would hear me. Then, out of nowhere I saw something flying towards me; it was my friend the hawk and he landed right on the top of the fence, turned his head sideways and looked right at me. We stared at each other for several seconds and I was about to tell him about Ginger when we heard a rustling in a bush, which immediately got both our attention. Out crawled the iguana. What was amazing to me was not only that the hawk didn't fly right over to him and scare him away, but that they should both appear at the same time! How did they know I needed them?

I started barking at them both to tell them how unhappy I was that Ginger was gone; and just when we were starting to be friends. None of us knew what to do and I was about to just go back into the house with dad, when we saw a cloud of dust coming straight towards us from up on the ridge. It was approaching really fast and you could hear pounding on the ground and then we all saw it; a giant mass of scraggly fur belonging to none other than Milo. He came to a screeching halt right at the fence, almost flipping himself forward from the quick stop, and he started barking at me. I don't know how, for certain, but he knew. We all understood. We had to find Ginger. And so we gathered together, all of us, to develop a plan.

Milo would dig a hole under the fence so I could get out, and while he could run far and fast, I would attempt to keep up as much as possible. We would then search every yard, all around the ridge and even look through the woods and park in our effort to find Ginger. The hawk, on the other hand, with his excellent eyesight, would soar through the sky looking for anything that moved and he vowed to find her and then come tell us where she was. And the iguana, with his amazing water skills, would swim through every pool in the neighborhood, every lake, puddle and pond, to assist in our search.

It was a good plan, and even though I knew mom and dad would be upset when they couldn't find me, I knew it would all be worth it in the end. We just had to find Ginger and I needed her to know that this was her home and that it was safe here and that I would love and accept her, help her and be there for her no matter what.

So off went the hawk and the iguana, as Milo began digging under the fence with all his might; grass, dirt and pebbles flying everywhere.

While watching Milo dig, I began to think about how amazing my new friends were, with their genuine caring and eagerness to help find Ginger. And seeing Milo willing to go to great lengths to search for his friend, made me realize that there were much more important things in life than just wanting to be the center of attention. What mattered were good friends and especially, a special sister like Ginger who needed me.

10

It hurt a lot when I tore out a chunk of my fur trying to get
out from under the fence but I shook it off, not wanting to
slow down our search. Once I was clear of the fence, Milo
took off at top speed and I pushed my aging body to keep
up with him the best that I could.   For starters, we ran
behind every house that backed up to the ridge looking for
any movement or sign. Hold on Ginger.......we're coming to
find you!

Never being out on my own, except for the one time I tried
to run away, it was exciting but a little scary too. There
were so many new smells and sites to see. Milo and I knew
we were heading in the right direction because we picked
up Ginger's scent.   You see dogs and people have the same
three senses; seeing, hearing and smelling.   But a dog's
sense of smell is 1,000 to 10,000 times more sensitive. And
when we lick our nose when it's dry, we are sometimes just
trying to smell things better.

After hours of searching under the heat of the afternoon sun, we decided to try and find a shady spot to rest and cool off. Milo plopped down hard right under the shade of a tree but I had to dig a bit of a hole in the dirt to make my spot as cool as possible.

While drifting off to sleep, thinking of finding Ginger, I was hit with a hard, wet spray of water and an angry lady yelling at us to "get out of here!" Jumping up and running as hard and fast as I could, Milo over took me with ease. I guess we picked the wrong yard to rest in!

The sun began to set and thankfully it was cooling off a little so we agreed to keep moving on for a while longer. But as darkness came, so did our hunger pangs. We never even thought about food when we left on our journey.

Finding a puddle of water, most likely left over from someone's sprinklers, we drank. About to give up finding any food, and just as we crossed a road into an unfamiliar neighborhood, we both were hit with it at the same time. We followed the scent and ……….jackpot! Someone was cooking steaks on a grill.

We had to think fast, and did. The plan was for Milo, who was much faster than me, to run and grab those steaks off the grill when the man went back into the house which we watched him do once or twice.

Milo crouched down getting into position and just as the man turned away from the grill heading into the house, Milo sprang into action. It was a great plan and I could almost taste it. He reached the grill, grabbed onto the piece of steak and was in the process of pulling it off the grill when the door flung open and Milo and the man were face to face. Get out of there I barked to Milo and he dropped the steak on the ground and turned to run, but stopped in his tracks when he heard a kind voice say "come here boy. Are you hungry?" So Milo stopped, eager to trust this person offering food.

His judgement was good because the man came over, pat Milo on the head, and proceeded to take the steak, clean it off, and cut it into bite sized pieces on a paper plate. I couldn't stand it.........I had to get some of that steak, so I stepped out into the open and slowly walked over to where they were. Sure enough, I also got a scratch behind my ears, which I loved, and then I too, got a plate of cut up meat.

After our great meal, a bowl of fresh water was set down for us and a blanket was laid out, close to the house in a protected nook. Without hesitation, we took a long drink of the water and then curled up together on the soft blanket, thanking this kind man with our eyes and then fell fast asleep. I dreamed of eating all the steak I wanted and was grateful for this kind person. I am really going to try and be nicer.........especially to Ginger when we find her. Maybe if I was nicer to her from the start she wouldn't have gone away.

Lost in a deep sleep, my eyes shot open when I felt something crawling on me. It was big and heavy............oh, what is it? I jumped up and saw it was a snake! And as I leaped higher than even I thought I could, I started hopping around trying desperately to get the snake off of me. In all the excitement Milo woke up, saw what was happening, jumped up and grabbed the snake in his mouth and flung it far into the bushes. I was so frightened and didn't want to chance the snake coming back so we decided to get out of there.

I wish we could have thanked the nice man but it was time to move on.

As we were walking, I couldn't help but think about Ginger and how she was so sweet and caring to her friends Milo and Daisy and how she sat so patiently with the little boy in the special chair. And now Milo and my new friends were helping in the search for her, we met a nice man who took us in and fed us giving us a safe and warm place to rest........it finally hit me. I needed to be nicer to everyone, whoever they were, and not only think about myself.

I was quickly snapped back to the present hearing lots of unfamiliar sounds. There were loud cries, croaking, chirping and buzzing sounds and as I moved closer to Milo I heard fluttering of wings and landing right in front of us was our friend, the hawk. He reported that he had been searching high and low and there was no sign of Ginger. He was tired and going to find shelter in a tree and rest for a while, so we thanked him and moved on.

11

The green iguana, a large fellow measuring over four and a half feet in length, was busy eating plants and an occasional flower, when he was lucky enough to find one. He has razor sharp teeth and a sharp tail, both used to drive off predators. And should he find the need to detach his tail, which was half of his body length, to escape, he simply grew back another one.

After a good breakfast, the iguana decided to find a nice sunny spot to warm up and rest. He just loved the hot, sunny weather.

Everything was unfamiliar now. After walking for days through the woods, we heard the sound of water and rounding a tangle of dead branches, we saw that we were at a large canal. There was nowhere to go except back into the woods or across the canal and there was no way for us to cross except for a very narrow bridge. It was actually more like a rotting board. Milo and I glanced at each other, back at the canal and then at each other again. We knew what we had to do.

Milo decided to go first and started out at almost a crawl, testing his weight on the board. I watched him moving slowly, wood creaking with every step when suddenly there was a big splash. At first I thought it was Milo falling into the water, but soon realized that something was moving straight for him………and moving fast.

We saw the beady little eyes surface and then the large jaws of an alligator begin to stretch open. Poor Milo was trying with all his might to move quicker across the broken down board and no sooner did I think it was all over for him, out of nowhere came the iguana who quickly bit on the tail of the alligator causing him to turn, taking his attention off Milo, who at this point was frozen in one spot unable to move. The iguana then swam to the front of the alligator and bit him again, swimming in the opposite direction of where we were, causing the alligator to take a sharp turn in pursuit.

I did chuckle to myself as Milo began to hop across the make shift bridge, sort of like a rabbit in fast motion. But he made it………he was on the other side. I closed my eyes, after realizing our friend was doing a great job distracting the alligator, took a deep breath to gather my courage, then ran across the board hoping I wouldn't fall through one of the rotting holes or have it collapse all together.

We were reunited once again and, as we looked down the length of the canal, our friend looked back at us and, seeing we were safe, proceeded to dart right up the bank of the canal and straight up a tree. That'll teach the alligator to mess with us!

12

We were very tired after our ordeal with the alligator. Finding a soft patch of ground covered in leaves, we decided to rest. I never knew I could sleep with one eye open, which I did, just to make sure nothing decided to crawl my way and scare me.

Milo and I stood and had a good stretch after a nap and my first thought was that mom and dad must be really worried and I was missing them. First, Ginger goes missing and then I disappear. Maybe not the smartest thing for me to do but I'm hoping they will understand and be happy when I show up back home with Ginger by my side.

Ginger....where are you? Please be okay.

13

Being a bird of prey, the hawk was busy looking for small rodents and frogs to eat while, at the same time, searching for Ginger. With his sharp talons, large curved bill and strong legs, not to mention his exceptional eyesight, he had little trouble finding and catching his food. Not only can a hawk see colors, but he can dive 150 miles per hour and catch his prey in midair.

After a busy morning of hunting, he decided to land on a top branch of a tree and look around for any possible movement.......you never knew if Ginger might be nearby.

The sun was warm and Milo and I were getting hungry and very thirsty. The trick was going to be finding food as there were no houses in sight.

We drank from a muddy puddle and, while I can't say it tasted very good, I was grateful for something wet to ease my thirst.

Nose to the ground, I followed behind Milo as we searched for anything edible. Checking out what looked like some interesting berries, we took a taste and decided to stay away from them. Sometimes you just have to follow your instincts. We soon picked up the scent of something definitely worthy of further investigation and it came from under a bush so we followed it. We discovered the remains of a fresh kill; maybe a rat or a squirrel, hard to tell.

Now I'm not saying I was overly thrilled to eat a raw dead animal, but when you are as hungry as we were, you're willing to try all sorts of things.

Milo grabbed one end and I the other and we pulled. We were each able to get a decent bite of whatever it was but no more than that. It seemed to quiet down the loud gurgling in my stomach. At least for the moment it did.

Continuing to sniff the area in hopes of finding another morsel of food, from out of nowhere came a hand lashing out at us, followed by a scream and a hiss. I jumped back terrified, but Milo wasn't so lucky. The hand, with the long nails, caught him right across his nose causing him to cry out in pain before he was able to move away. Out came a very angry raccoon, definitely looking for a fight and it kept hissing at us showing teeth and swiping at us with his long nails. It wasn't easy to get away as there were downed tree branches, bushes and sharp prickly sticks, all close together and I kept getting my paws stuck, losing my balance trying to get them off.

Milo was growling at the raccoon but at the same time, he was pawing at his face and nose. I knew it hurt him a lot and there was blood trickling down his snout.

The raccoon kept charging him and swiping at him, catching him a few more times. I tried running behind the raccoon and was barking at it, with no effect. I doubted it could even hear me above his high pitched screams and Milo's growling. And just as the raccoon was about to charge Milo yet again, I heard a loud, hoarse screaming sound from up above.

KEE-EEEEEEEEE-ARR

Diving straight down from high in the sky was none other than our friend, the Hawk. Again, he screamed, KEE-EEEEEEEEEEEEEE-ARR and then held his huge wings straight out to the sides and stretched out his powerful legs, reached down, grabbing the raccoon, and carried him away.

We couldn't believe our eyes, or our luck, but I quickly ran over to Milo to check out his wounds. He had gashes to the side of his neck as well as the one on his nose and all I could think to do was to try and lick away some of the blood and tell him how brave he was and that he would be okay.

No sooner did Milo begin to shake the pain away, our friend the Hawk reappeared to check on us. As we were about to tell him about how we happened upon the raccoon, I heard slight chirping sounds coming from way under some brush and, of course, I had to go investigate. To my complete surprise, I saw two baby raccoons, calling out to their mother.

Oh no, what had we done. It all began to make sense. It was a mother raccoon trying to protect her babies and not only did we pose a threat, but we ate their dinner. I quickly turned to the Hawk and begged him to go and bring back the mother raccoon so she could be reunited with her babies.

He flew away only to return moments later with a freshly caught squirrel and went and placed it near the baby raccoons. Then off again he went, coming back this time with a screaming mother raccoon. It appeared she was ready to turn on us again, once she was placed near her babies, but quickly realized there was fresh food for them all. We stood staring at each other for a moment, as she realized we were not there to hurt her or her babies. She blinked a few times then turned, picked up the gift we left for her and disappeared. I felt bad for Milo because I knew his cuts were hurting him but, I also had a warm, happy feeling come over me. It felt good to help the raccoon and her family and to understand that the mother was only doing what every mother would have done………protect her children.

And I was going to protect Ginger once we found her because, you see, we are family and families look out for one another and love each other.

14

Days turned into weeks and Milo and I were exhausted and getting weak from lack of much food. The Iguana and the Hawk would appear periodically to check in with us but had no news about Ginger. Thankfully the Hawk would bring us a small rodent on occasion which was the only reason we were able to go on at all.

I was beginning to give up all hope of ever finding Ginger and I just wanted to go home and curl up on the sofa with my pillows and get hugs from mom and dad and feel safe. And sleep.

After an entire day and night of rain mixed with thunder and lightning (I could only think about poor Ginger and how upset she must be), we saw a clearing of clouds in the sky and the sun broke through, so we decided to move on. We came across a dirt road so followed it. Soon we heard a rumbling and turned to see a pick-up truck coming towards us. We quickly jumped off the road and hid as it passed us by. While I kept thinking of home, and a ride in that truck would probably get me there, we felt we needed to play it safe. We had come so far to give up now.

We were grateful for all the trees, as they provided some much needed shade. The sun was out and with the heat rising up from the drenched ground; it was beginning to feel like we were in a sauna.

Every bone in our bodies was aching from exhaustion. Milo looked at me, and I at him, and we hardly recognized each other anymore. My beautiful, fluffy, well-groomed coat was a mass of knots and was matted with dried mud, not to mention I had fleas now and probably a few ticks. Milo, though always a bit scraggly, but in a very cute way, was now a heap of twisted, dirty and smelly hair and I could barely see his eyes anymore.

Turning off the road, finding a cool spot to lay and rest for the night, we both sighed and groaned as we lay down on a patch of leaves and then both quickly fell fast asleep.

I was awakened sometime during the night, and heard what sounded like dogs barking off in the distance. I lay very still, listening hard, trying to drown out all the night noises of insects and critters. Sure enough, that's what it was. Dogs barking. I looked over at Milo, who was so deep in sleep he was actually snoring. Instead of waking him up, I decided to leave him be. Getting up, a quick stretch, I was off to investigate.

It was never easy travelling through the thick brush, and I knew we were close to the dirt road, so I chose that as my path. It was dark and very still, and a little scary too, going by myself. Stopping every so often to listen carefully, I was definitely getting closer to the sounds of the barking dogs, and my nose told me the same.

While all puppies are born unable to hear until they are about 21 days old, our hearing is stronger than people, but not as strong as our sense of smell or our eyesight. So I could smell the dogs, and the many muscles in my ears allowed me to turn them in various directions to help me hear them in the distance better.

But what's this? It looks like a dirt driveway and it curved into the trees. There was a rotting, wooden post with a mailbox sitting on top of it, which looked like it would crumble to dust any minute but I knew I was close to where the barking dogs were so I had to go down that path. As I made the turn, I heard a rumbling coming up behind me so I quickly jumped off the road and hid. Peering out from behind the tall weeds and grass, I saw the same old pick-up truck and again, it drove past me, kicking up dirt and dust as it went. I wasn't sure if I should continue down this path as the dogs that were barking might be his, and I didn't have a good feeling about the driver of this truck.

I stayed where I was and, before long, I heard the truck come to a stop, the engine die and then the slamming of a metal door. The dogs really started barking then and it got quite loud when I heard a man's voice yell for them to shut up. It got quiet except for, what sounded like rattling cages. Staying safely hidden for a while, my curiosity finally got the best of me and I just had to go see what was going on.

There were overgrown tree branches hanging on the road and a lot of pot holes, some still filled with water from the last rains. I walked what seemed like a long time when I finally came to a clearing where I saw an old house with peeling paint and the old pick-up truck parked out front. There were lights on and I could smell something cooking which reminded me of how hungry I was.

Looking around the yard, I saw some old rusted out cars and other items I couldn't identify but then something else caught my eye. There was a dilapidated fence and it was from behind there that I could hear little cries of dogs and rattling of cages. Carefully walking around the fence, I was hit by both shock and horror. There, before me, was cage upon cage, stacked 5 and 6 high, row after row all filled with dogs. It was hard to know just how many there were. I froze in place as all eyes seemed to turn to look at me, pleading for help. I shook off my fear and slowly began to check each and every cage and I knew. Ginger was here.

As I began walking among the cages, many of the dogs started to bark so I lay down as flat to the ground as I could and tried to make them understand they needed to be quiet. As they all began to settle, I looked back towards the fence and, realizing, that no one was coming, I continued my search. There were so many dogs and they were living in filthy cages with no water and they looked even hungrier than I felt. They were in all shapes and sizes, smaller ones cramped together in cages and the larger dogs could barely stand as their cages were too small for them. I wanted to help every one of them but I had to look for Ginger first. So I went cage by cage, row by row, slowly looking up at each one hoping to see my sister, Ginger.

About half way through one of the rows of cages, and without any warning, I was grabbed from behind by the scruff of my neck and yanked up off my feet. I was squirming and kicking and biting, trying to get free from the hand that held me but without any luck. I was then carried down toward the end of the row of cages and thrown into one with three other dogs.

15

I didn't know if they were angry I was there, or happy to see me at first; they all started jumping on me and biting my ears and my tail. It brought back memories of the place I came from so I quickly turned to each of the three dogs and nipped back making sure they knew I was in control here.

It turned out that they were just really happy to see me and had gotten overly excited. I don't think any of them had ever been taught manners which I kind of understood, as it looked like they had been there for a pretty long time. Once they all settled down, it hit me. I was stuck in this cage too, and what was I going to do? How was I going to find Ginger and bring her home? I started to bark as loudly as I could, though who would hear me with my hoarse, raspy voice.

But wait.........I heard a dog crying and it sounded like her. I'm sure of it. I shuffled from side to side, looking from cage to cage, and there she was. I saw her. It was my Ginger.

And she saw me and I was trying to say everything I had been thinking and wanting to say over these last weeks. I love you Ginger, I barked, and I promise that, no matter what, I will always take care of you and protect you and help you. Now, I just had to figure out how to get us both out of here.

She looked so happy to see me but she was so thin and weak and very dirty. I became more determined to get her out of this awful place and started biting on the door of the cage. I twisted and turned my head but just couldn't seem to grab onto it. I thought I was getting close when I heard voices and banging on the cages, sending all the dogs into a fury of barking and yelping, and it appeared there were several men opening each cage, throwing something in quickly and then slamming the doors shut. When they got to my cage, I was ready. The hand appeared and I bit down as hard as I could only to get a slap across my head, sending me right down, and the door slammed shut.

By the time I could shake it off and get back on my feet, I realized it was food that had been thrown in the cage, and not in a bowl or anything. And it was all gone. The other three dogs ate it all, with no thought to saving some for me but, I knew how hungry they must have been and probably needed it more than me. Glancing over to Ginger, I was so happy that she managed to get her share.

The hours passed slowly and Ginger and I kept sending loving, yet frightened, whimpers and cries to each other in the dark, and I kept promising her I would figure a way out of this. Hunger, frustration and exhaustion finally getting the best of me, I fell into a deep sleep.

16

My eyes shot open with a start when I heard something moving close by as the other three dogs were practically crawling under my coat trying to hide. Straining to try and see where it was coming from, I almost jumped out of my own skin as something large, hairy and very smelly was staring back at me from outside my cage. I closed my eyes as tight as I could as if I could wish it away. Or maybe I just thought I saw something. Oh, but the smell. And something was now on top of my cage and it was scratching as if it wanted to get in and get us. All of us were terrified but I finally opened my eyes, ready to do my part to protect the others when I looked up and just couldn't believe my eyes. There was Milo, staring back at me. And the Iguana was scratching at the wire of the cage from above. By some miracle they had found me. And by finding me, they found Ginger too.

The Hawk had flown into our last resting place, bringing food, when Milo realized I wasn't there. So, with his help, they were able to find me. And there was water nearby, so the Iguana was happy to join in the rescue.

While listening to Milo's story, I kept trying to interrupt him to tell him the great news. We found Ginger! And when I finally got it out, he started leaping in the air and spinning, begging me to tell him where she was. As I directed him to her, he ran over and trying to reach her cage, leaped in the air to get a glimpse of her, crying to her in his utter excitement.

Okay, okay. Enough of that! There were bad men here and we had to plan our escape quickly. The dogs were all starting to get restless and I was so afraid they would start barking, when the Hawk flew in, with his wings spread wide, landing right in the middle of all the cages. It immediately became so quiet you could hear a pin drop. I'm sure it was out of fear but it worked. There was silence.

The Iguana got busy and went to work very quickly unlatching the door to my cage with his long nails and no sooner did he get it opened, I jumped out without giving a thought to the fall or to the fact that the three dogs with me would jump out after me and use me as a cushion.. They took off immediately and I never saw them again. I hope they are okay.

The Iguana then quickly made it over to Ginger's cage and opened the door. Although I could see the fear in her eyes about the long distance to the ground, Milo and I reassured her we would be there to help her and keep her safe.

The fall did knock the wind out of her a bit, but the kisses and snuggles she got from me and Milo I think made up for it. We just couldn't get enough of each other and I heard her cry but it was joy not fear this time. I promised I would be the best big sister and love her and help her through her difficult times, like all the noises she was always afraid of.

The Hawk quickly brought us all back to reality and urged us to move on and get as far away from this awful place as we could. We gathered up Ginger and turned to leave when I stopped in my tracks and looked back at all the dogs still in their cages, their eyes pleading with me. How can we leave all these dogs here I asked? Without another word or direction, the Iguana leaped into action and began opening cages with great speed. The Hawk actually grabbed hold of the smallest dogs that were high up in cages and gently placed them on the ground. Soon there were dogs everywhere and Milo and I could only try and keep them quiet.

When they were all free, Milo, Ginger and I took off at once following the lead of the Hawk, and the Iguana promised to meet up with us again soon.

We didn't dare go back onto the dirt road for fear the men in the pickup truck would realize that we were gone and track us down. We warned Ginger that it would be difficult, travelling through the wooded area, but I stayed very close to her and went first to create openings through all the branches and vines. Every so often I just had to stop and nuzzle up to her………I still couldn't believe we had found her.

The bushes behind me started to rustle and I was afraid it was the men coming to look for us. Could we out run them?

Milo picked up on my fear and ran to my side, ready to take them on. Slowly, crawling low to the ground in a submissive way, were a few of the dogs we had freed. With a sigh of relief, we let them know they were safe with us. And as they stood to join us, more and more dogs stepped out from behind the bushes. There had to be about 20 of them, all looking to join us in our escape.

17

We trudged through the night and into the next day to get as far away as we could from that horrible place. I couldn't help think about the kind of person that would want to have dogs and then keep them in cages all the time and not take care of them? Dogs should not be left alone, like in that place. We need to be with our families and get lots of love and attention.

Walking until the heat of the afternoon sun became more than we could bear, we decided to look for a shady place that would fit all of us. The Iguana appeared and happily led us to a small lake and, no sooner did we see it, all twenty three of us ran and jumped right in. And just like that, we all began to swim and play and act like dogs having the best time, all friends, and none of us was thinking of the horrible place or any of the bad things that happened to us. Even the Iguana joined in the fun, though he had to be very careful not to hit any of us with his long, powerful tail. My heart was especially happy because, even with all Ginger's fears, she was actually having fun in the water and you could see how happy she and Milo were to be together again. I started to feel a slight pang of jealousy watching them splash in the water together when Ginger stopped, turned to look at me, and trotted over rubbing her head against mine, and we both walked out of the water to the edge of the lake and lay down together more content than either of us had been in a very long time.

As the sun was setting, we were all exhausted from our play time and, while extremely hungry, we took comfort in the fact that we were together and so, we settled down under some bushes, staying close, and for the first time in weeks, I really slept. Ginger safely by my side.

18

Morning came and as we all began to wake and take big long stretches, none other than the Hawk showed up and he had breakfast. It was quite obvious he had been very successful on his recent hunt, and making numerous trips, he first brought food to Ginger and then came back time and again, feeding all the dogs saving me and Milo for last. We all ate hungrily and I managed to save a portion of mine which I pushed over towards Ginger. With our bellies satisfied, we all took a last swim and frolic in the lake and the last of the dirt and grime seemed to wash away which felt wonderful.

Gathering all the dogs, we laid out the plan and decided to head east. Once we made it to the road, we soon heard the sound of a car coming so, as planned, all hid. We couldn't be too careful not knowing if the men in the pickup truck were still after us or if another mean person would be in the car.

We travelled this road for several days, not seeing too many cars but always grateful for the afternoon sun showers as it provided puddles of water for us to quench our thirst. We hadn't seen the Iguana so knew we were not close to any water now. Food was almost nonexistent and all felt the pangs of hunger again. Ginger was really starting to show signs of weakness, as were many of the others, so we slowed our pace and stopped to rest more often. We were down to fifteen dogs now, five of the larger dogs deciding to go off on their own after our swim at the lake. We wished them well and prayed for their safety. While the others rested, Milo and I were trying to figure out our next move. Keep travelling down this road or maybe head off into the wooded area. This was all new territory to us, so we decided to stay on the road for a while longer, hoping something would start to look or smell familiar. I had to get Ginger home soon and start nursing her back to health. She tried so hard to be brave, but I knew; she was getting weaker by the day. She was even too exhausted to let the daily rain showers get her upset.

While all the dogs were resting, the Hawk flew to us with the news that he saw someone on the side of the road, so Milo and I decided to go check it out. Sure enough, as we peeked out from the tall grass, there was a woman walking a rather large dog. Seeing her reminded me of my mom, and I whimpered to myself, missing her and her loving touch. I decided to be brave and stepped out onto the road and walked right up to her, not even knowing if the big dog was friendly or not.

He was! And he came right over to me and, as we sniffed at each other, the woman gasped at seeing me and began talking to me in a familiar sweet, loving, almost baby talk way. "You poor baby" she said. "Just look at you. Are you lost?" She squatted down next to me and patted my head ever so gently and looked at the tag I still had around my neck. "Well, Chloe, you are a long way from home little girl, aren't you?" She whispered. "How would you like to go home?"

19

❋✦❀✦❀✦❀✦❀✦❀✦❀✦❀✦❀✦❀✦❀✦

Home. The word sounded so wonderful and brought back memories of mom and dad, of a loving, safe place, and just where I wanted to be. So, I kissed her hand as my way of saying yes, of course I want to go home. Please take me there.

After walking her dog back to, what looked like, a little house on wheels, she placed him inside and then came back over to where I was still standing and as she was about to pick me up, I ran back over towards the side of the road and started barking. Out came Milo and now the woman really looked surprised. "So, there are two of you", she said. "Well, that's just fine because we have plenty of room." And with that, I ran in a few circles (just like Ginger used to) and then took off into the woods to get Ginger and the others.

I ran first to Ginger and woke her up, telling her we found our way home and soon, all the others were up and following me and before you knew it, all of us were standing, looking up at this amazing woman who was going to take us home. Her eyes darted from one to the other, taking in our large group with her mouth partially open as if in disbelief. She approached us and Ginger and a few of the others immediately backed away in fear. After reassuring them it was safe, they came forward and one by one, began picking each one of us up, placing us in her house on wheels.

In a flash, bowls of fresh, clean water began to appear followed by paper plates of bologna, turkey and even some dog food. It was heaven.

Once she got us all settled in the back, she walked up to the front of her vehicle, started the engine and off we went. I could hear her on the phone and soon heard my name.   As I looked around at all the dogs, thirst quenched and bellies full for the first time in a very long time, I noticed there was a narrow couch on one side and it had pillows! I was so tempted but instead got up and moved close to the woman up front, followed by Milo and Ginger and we all curled up together. Milo and I took turns kissing and nuzzling Ginger.

20

From somewhere far away, I heard my name called and
then Ginger's. It was coming closer and became more
frantic. Shaking off sleep, trying to remember where I was,
it hit me.

The door was flung open, Ginger and I were scooped up and
we were in the arms of mom and dad and being covered
with kisses and hugs and they were both crying and we
were now safe, our nightmare over. They sat on the floor
and none of us could contain our excitement and relief to
be together and even Milo had to get in the action. This
was the happiest I had ever seen Ginger and for sure, it was
the happiest I had been in a very long time.

The other dogs were now alert, some running over to mom
and dad trying to get some of the love while others were
shy and stayed back. This went on for some time; all the
while the adults were talking about what to do with all
these dogs. It was then decided that some would stay with

us until good homes could be found and the rest would go with this wonderful woman.

Saying good-bye was not easy but I helped the others understand that their life was going to be wonderful from now on and who knows; maybe we would see each other again someday.

As the house on wheels drove off, I felt a pang of sadness; a part of me was going to miss those dogs. But I was proud of myself, too, for becoming the caring and loving girl that I had, and I did a good thing by finding Ginger and saving them all. Nothing was greater than walking back into our home, with all the warm smells, our beds still in place and MY PILLOWS! Oh how I missed them.

Dad gave Milo a big hug and put him on a leash, ready to walk him home to see his family, when we both stopped and looked at each other for a long time. It is difficult to explain the bond that had been created between us, all for the love of Ginger. We nuzzled together for a moment and I tried to find a way to thank him for all he had done. I knew he was anxious to go home to his family, so we said our good-byes, knowing we would see a lot of each other.

Mom arranged all the dogs in a separate area of the house, laid out blankets, fresh water and some food. Then Ginger and I were immediately checked from head to toe before being given a bath. And this time, neither of us minded. After lots more hugging, brushes and kisses, Ginger and I both curled up together on the sofa and I pushed my favorite pillow over towards her so we could share. We slept……. together.

Days passed and life couldn't get any better than this. All the dogs had been bathed and checked out by Doc Joyce, and all found their own loving, forever homes. Some we knew we would see again as their new homes were with friends of mom and dad.

Now, don't get me wrong; it was great being home and we were so much closer, but Ginger still had some of her problems with loud noises and running in circles barking, but it was me who stepped in now to try and comfort her. And we spent time together out in the yard, with mom watching us the whole time. Ginger even got to thank the Hawk and the Iguana personally, as they appeared one morning and couldn't be happier that we were together, safe at home.

21

Curled up together on the sofa one afternoon, sharing my pillow, we were awakened by mom's car pulling in the driveway. As always, we jumped up and run to the door to greet her, stopping in our tracks when we heard something unfamiliar. We stood together, looking at the door as it swung open and there was mom. But she wasn't alone.

Oh boy……….here we go again.

Chloe waiting for her friends

My handsome Skylar

The day we met Ginger.

Chloe.

Loving her pillow.

True love.

Ginger.

Milo

Chloe sleeping

My happy Ginger today

Made in the USA
Middletown, DE
17 January 2016